Carla Gets a Pet

Written by Robert R O'Brien

Illustrated by Mary Beth Schwark

Silver Burdett Ginn
A Division of Simon & Schuster
160 Gould Street
Needham Heights, MA 02194-2310

Design and production by Kirchoff/Wohlberg, Inc.

ISBN 0-663-59391-3

2 3 4 5 6 7 8 9 10 SP 01 00 99 98 97 96

"Mom, can I get a pet?" said Carla.
"What kind of a pet, Carla?" said Mom.

"I really want a dog," said
Carla. "A dog with soft fur and a
long tail. Please?"

"A pet is a lot of work, Carla," said Mom. "A dog needs to be fed and walked and kept safe. But if you show me you can take care of a pet, then you may have a dog."

Carla knew just what to do! She made a sign.

Pet
Care
by Carla. if
you need help with
a Dog —
call me

Carla waited for someone to call.
R-r-ring! At last, the phone rang. Carla
jumped up.

It was Mrs. Cook on the phone.
Mrs. Cook had hurt her leg. She said she
needed Carla to walk her dog. Carla said
she could help tomorrow.

When Carla got to Mrs. Cook's house, she saw a dog just like the one she wanted. He had a long tail and soft fur.

"This is King," said Mrs. Cook.
"I'm sure you two will be good
friends. Just don't let him chase cats."

Carla went outside with King. Carla
felt good! She could take care of a pet!

All of a sudden, King pulled hard on
the leash. Carla had to let go. Off ran
King, chasing a cat.

Carla ran after him and called,
"King! Come back! Stop!" But it was no
use. King was gone.

Carla looked everywhere. She'd
stop now and then to call. "King! Come
back! Where are you?" But no King.

Carla needed help. She saw her mom and called out to her. "Mom, I lost King. I feel bad. I did try to take care of him. Can you help me find him?"

Carla and her mom called and
called for King. They looked for him for
over an hour. But all they found was
King's leash.

Carla called Mrs. Cook. She had to tell her that King was lost. "I'm really sorry. I did try to take care of him, but he got away. I looked and looked, but all I found was his leash."

Mrs. Cook said, "Please come back to my house. We will talk about what to do."

Carla walked back to Mrs. Cook's
house with King's leash. She felt sad. She
had lost Mrs. Cook's pet.

When she got to the house, there was
King! "King, you came back!" said Carla.
Mrs. Cook smiled and said, "King is
not lost."

19

Mrs. Cook said, "Carla, you were a big help. You did try your best to take care of King. And you did just the right thing! You called to tell me that King was lost."

"I'm glad King came back," said Carla.

The next day, Carla's mom took her
to the pet store. Carla began to think
about a dog with a long tail and soft fur.

She began to think about King—and
what her mom had said about taking care
of pets. And when Carla came out of the
store, she had her very own . . .

pet goldfish!

"A dog is too much work!" said Carla.